The Great Big
Enormous Turnip

THE GREAT BIG
ENORMOUS
TURNIP

Pictures by
HELEN OXENBURY
Story by
ALEXEI TOLSTOY

FRANKLIN WATTS, INC.
845 Third Avenue, New York, N.Y. 10022

First published in England 1968
by William Heinemann Ltd

First American publication 1968
by Franklin Watts, Inc.

Library of Congress Catalog Card Number 69–10277
Illustrations © Helen Oxenbury 1968

watts
INTERNATIONAL

Printed in Great Britain by
Colour Reproductions Limited

Once upon a time an old man planted
a little turnip and said,
"Grow, grow, little turnip, grow sweet. Grow,
grow, little turnip, grow strong."

And the turnip grew up sweet and strong, and big and enormous.
Then, one day, the old man went to pull it up.
He pulled and pulled again, but he could not pull it up.

He called the old woman.

The old woman pulled the old man.
The old man pulled the turnip.
And they pulled and pulled again, but they
could not pull it up.

So the old woman called her granddaughter.

The granddaughter pulled the old woman,
The old woman pulled the old man,
The old man pulled the turnip.
And they pulled and pulled again, but they
could not pull it up.

The granddaughter called
the black dog.

The black dog pulled the granddaughter,
The granddaughter pulled the old woman,
The old woman pulled the old man,
The old man pulled the turnip.
And they pulled and pulled again, but they
could not pull it up.

The black dog called the cat.

The cat pulled the dog.
The dog pulled the granddaughter,
The granddaughter pulled the old woman,
The old woman pulled the old man,
The old man pulled the turnip.
And they pulled and pulled again, but still they
could not pull it up.

The cat called the mouse.

The mouse pulled the cat,
The cat pulled the dog,
The dog pulled the granddaughter,
The granddaughter pulled the old woman,
The old woman pulled the old man,
The old man pulled the turnip.

They pulled and pulled again, and up
came the turnip at last.